Elsie's Selfies

T0337100

Written by Jane Clarke

Illustrated by Mike Phillips

Collins

Who and what is in this story?

Listen and say

photo

Grandma

Pop the parrot

Elsie

There was a photo of Elsie at her grandma's house. It was on the wall in the hall. It was a photo of Elsie and Grandma's parrot, Pop.

"Look, you're a beautiful baby," said Grandma.

"I'm not a baby now," said Elsie. "Let's take a new photo. I can use my tablet."

Elsie went into the garden. She stood in the sun with Pop on her shoulder.

"Don't move, Pop," Elsie said to the parrot. "We're taking a selfie."

The sun was in Elsie's eyes. The photo was bad.

Let's try again, Pop.

This time, Elsie stood under a tree in the shade. Pop saw a parrot on the screen.

Elsie was angry with Pop.

"Pop! I want a photo of both of us!" she said.

Elsie put Pop in the tree. She tried again. "Smile, please, Pop," she said. "One, two, three ..." Pop tried to eat Elsie's ear!

The photo was bad again!

"Pop!" Elsie said. "Let's try again."

Elsie tried again by the house. There was not much sun and Pop sat on her shoulder. But then Grandma said, "Do you want a drink, Elsie?"

Elsie turned her head to speak
to Grandma.

Oh no!

"Did you take a good photo for me?" asked Grandma.

"No! All the photos are bad," Elsie said.

15

"Show me the photos, Elsie," said Grandma.

"OK," said Elsie. Elsie showed Grandma all the photos.

Elsie looked at the photos again.

Look! What's that, Grandma?

Grandma looked at the photos again. "A cat," she said. "I can see a cat in all your photos. It's the lost cat!"

Grandma and Elsie looked in the kitchen.

The cat was behind the bin. "Let's take the cat home," said Grandma. "I know where it lives."

"Can I come?" asked Elsie.

"Yes," said Grandma. "Elsie's selfies found the cat!"

Grandma, Elsie and Pop took the cat to its home.

"I have an idea," said Grandma. "Elsie, take a photo for my wall."

"Smile, everyone," said Elsie.

"What a great photo," said Grandma.

Picture dictionary

Listen and repeat

bin

lost

screen

selfie

shade

tablet

1 Look and order the story

2 Listen and say

Collins

Published by Collins
An imprint of HarperCollins*Publishers*
Westerhill Road
Bishopbriggs
Glasgow
G64 2QT

HarperCollins*Publishers*
1st Floor, Watermarque Building
Ringsend Road
Dublin 4
Ireland

William Collins' dream of knowledge for all began with the publication of his first book in 1819.

A self-educated mill worker, he not only enriched millions of lives, but also founded a flourishing publishing house. Today, staying true to this spirit, Collins books are packed with inspiration, innovation and practical expertise. They place you at the centre of a world of possibility and give you exactly what you need to explore it.

© HarperCollins*Publishers* Limited 2020

10 9 8 7 6 5 4 3 2

ISBN 978-0-00-839704-3

Collins® and COBUILD® are registered trademarks of HarperCollins*Publishers* Limited

www.collins.co.uk/elt

British Library Cataloguing in Publication Data

A catalogue record for this publication is available from the British Library.

Author: Jane Clarke
Illustrator: Mike Phillips (Beehive)
Series editor: Rebecca Adlard
Commissioning editor: Fiona Undrill
Publishing manager: Lisa Todd
Product managers: Jennifer Hall and Caroline Green
In-house editor: Alma Puts Keren
Project manager: Emily Hooton
Editor: Matthew Hancock
Proofreaders: Natalie Murray and Michael Lamb
Cover designer: Kevin Robbins
Typesetter: 2Hoots Publishing Services Ltd
Audio produced by id audio, London
Reading guide author: Emma Wilkinson
Production controller: Rachel Weaver
Printed and bound by: GPS Group, Slovenia

MIX
Paper from
responsible sources
FSC
www.fsc.org
FSC™ C007454

This book is produced from independently certified FSC™ paper to ensure responsible forest management.

For more information visit: **www.harpercollins.co.uk/green**

Download the audio for this book and a reading guide for parents and teachers at www.collins.co.uk/839704